Wash the Peas

PEAS

Pea Pancakes ← Yum

1 teacup of green peas
2 egg
milk
cream
4 tablespoons flour
½ teaspoon baking powder
½ teaspoon sugar
pinch of salt
4 tablespoons butter

Mash together → Blend
↓ Fry
Flip!!

tea break

Yes, Peas!

Pea Porridge

400g Peas

Mmmmmmm

Yummy Yummy
YUM.

FLIP.

# The Princess and the Peas

For Bob and Carole, with love ~ C. H.

For Lucy and Harry and the "Pea-sticks" ~ S. W.

Text copyright © 2012 by Caryl Hart
Illustrations copyright © 2012 by Sarah Warburton
Nosy Crow and its logos are trademarks of Nosy Crow Ltd. Used under license.

First U.S. edition 2013

Library of Congress Catalog Card Number 2012942408
ISBN 978-0-7636-6532-6

12 13 14 15 16 17 LRX 10 9 8 7 6 5 4 3 2 1

Printed in Dongguan, Guangdong, China
This book was typeset in ThrohandInk.
The illustrations were done in mixed media.

Nosy Crow
An imprint of Candlewick Press
99 Dover Street
Somerville, Massachusetts 02144

www.nosycrow.com
www.candlewick.com

# The Princess and the Peas

Caryl Hart

Sarah Warburton

to the PALACE

☒ no peas!

nosy crow

An imprint of Candlewick Press

Lily-Rose May was a sweet little girlie;
her eyes were bright blue and her hair was so curly.
She lived with her dad in a beautiful wood.
She was kind and polite and was usually good.

She did all her homework and cared for her rabbits.
She did not pick her nose or have other bad habits.
She kept her room neat and was eager to please,

UNTIL . . .

one day, her daddy tried feeding her peas.

When Lily-Rose May found the peas on her plate,
she worked herself into a terrible state.
"But, darling," said Dad, "can't you manage a few?
They're ever so tiny and SO good for you."

Lily ran out, her dinner uneaten.
But Dad was determined—
he wouldn't be beaten.

So he went to the library and brought home a book.

Then . . .

he pulled on his apron
and started to cook.

the DESPERATE
HOUSEWIFE
How to HIDE
Peas
& other
unsavory
VEGetables

He blended up peas
into smoothies and shakes.

He baked them in cookies
and put them in cakes.

He laid the food out
in a beautiful feast,
feeling sure Lily-Rose
would eat ONE pea, at least.

But Lily-Rose May said
it made her feel poorly.

Her hands were all sweaty.
Her skin felt so crawly.

"My tummy is churning.
Oh, turn the page quick!
I'm going to be terribly,
horribly sick!"

# The next day,

the doctor jumped out of his car,

shouting, "Lily-Rose May, open wide and say 'Ahh!' "

Then he listed her symptoms:
    *"Quite pretty, polite,*
*and allergic to peas."*
    He thought he was right.

"With all things considered, I have to assess,
this disease has no cure! The girl's a princess."
"You have to be joking!" her father exclaimed.
"She's a princess all right," the doctor explained.

And to prove it, he told them a terrible tale . . .

of a beautiful maiden caught up in a gale:

She came to the palace, all covered in snow, crying, "Please let me in. I'm a princess, you know."

To make sure the poor girl was telling the truth, the queen made a bed piled as high as the roof.

And right at the bottom, she snuck in a pea. Then she tucked the girl in, with a hot mug of tea.

"If the pea wakes her up,
we'll have a Royal Wedding.
No princess can sleep with a
pea in her bedding!"
The poor girl was terribly ill
all night through.
She did not sleep a wink.
She was bruised black and blue.

You see, **every** princess
is allergic to peas.
So she said to the queen,
"Do get rid of it, please!"
The queen was so sorry.
She vowed there and then,
to **never** have peas
in the palace again!

The doctor said, "That is why Lily-Rose May
should pack up and move to the palace today.
Even ONE pea might kill her. Now, pass me my hat."
Then he wrote out his bill . . .

and was gone.

Just like that.

Lily-Rose May gave her daddy a cuddle.
"Oh, what shall I do? I'm in such a big muddle!
I would so love to live at the palace—it's true.
But I want to stay here, in the forest with you."

"I know," soothed her dad,
"but the doctor knows best."
So they packed all her toys
and her clothes in a chest.

Then off to the palace went Lily-Rose May,
with a promise to write to her dad every day.

The queen said, "How lovely,
        a brand-new princess!
Here, have lots of jewels and
        a pretty new dress.
You'll find all you need
        up the stairs in your room.
Just make sure you come down
        to eat lunch at noon."

Lily-Rose's ROOM

DRESSING-UP ROOM

SHOE ROOM

Lily-Rose

This isn't so bad,
Lily thought with a smile.
I could manage to be
a princess for a while. . . .

I've got my own bathroom
and teddies galore . . .

and a whole ton of books!
What girl could want more?

So she put on her dress
and some fabulous shoes

and had great fun deciding
which earrings to choose.

She placed a tiara
on top of her head,
then switched on the TV
and bounced on the bed.

When the clock on the landing was striking midday,
Lily swept down to lunch in a princessy way.
"Ah, there you are, darling." The king and queen smiled.
"You're safe now—don't worry, you poor little child.

We know you've been having a terrible time.
Your own dad gave you **peas**! What a hideous crime.
But now you shall live like a proper princess.
Do you know what we're having for lunch? Can you guess?
Our very best chef made it
specially for you.
A lovely big bowl full of . . .

"Now, eat up your lunch,

then your training can start.

You've got fifty-four speeches
to learn by heart.

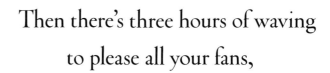
Then there's three hours of waving
to please all your fans,

and lessons in smiling,

and shaking of hands."

THREE HOURS of waving?
thought Lily-Rose May.

And bowls full of sloppy green
slush every day?

I thought living here would be oodles of fun,
but this is a nightmare! Oh, what have I done?

"I may **not** be a princess,"
    said Lily-Rose May.
"And I have to get home
        to my dad, right away!

I'm sure I can learn
        to eat peas if I try."
Then she gave back the jewels
    and said, "Thank you! Good-bye!"

Now Lily-Rose May is an expert in peas.

She just dips them in ketchup or chocolate or cheese.

Then she gobbles them up, as quick as can be . . .

and she NEVER goes back to the palace for tea.